Licensed exclusively to Top That Publishing Ltd
Tide Mill Way, Woodbridge, Suffolk, IP12 1AP, UK
www.topthatpublishing.com
Copyright © 2015 Sally Garland
All rights reserved
0 2 4 6 8 9 7 5 3 1
Manufactured in China

Written and Illustrated by Sally Garland

ISBN 978-1-78445-285-8

A catalogue record for this book is available from the British Library

'For Johnny and Chloe'

Tig & Tog
The Discovery

by Sally Garland

Tig didn't want Tog
to play with the stick.

It was her stick.

So she stomped away and sat alone, drawing in the snow with it.

Then Tig noticed something strange and
interesting sticking out of the ground.

She used her stick to scrape
and scratch the earth.

But the stick
wasn't enough!

She needed something else to
dig it out of the ground.

'What do you think it is?'

asked Tog.

Tog took a spoon out of his pocket
and he sat down to help Tig.

With the spoon, they scooped and ladled the earth. But it was no good.

The spoon wasn't enough!

They still needed something else to dig the thing out of the ground.

In the sandpit, Tig and Tog
found a little plastic spade.

With the little spade they dug and dug.

But even the spade wasn't enough!

They still needed something else
to dig the thing out of the ground.

Tig and Tog looked for
something else to help
them dig.

Looking around,
they saw a bucket
in a muddy puddle.

Tog pulled it out using the stick.

Tig and Tog took turns filling the bucket with earth and tipping it out.

But even the bucket wasn't enough!

They still needed something else to dig the thing out of the ground.

'Can you see
what it is yet?'

asked Tig.

'It's so
strange
and big!'

'It looks like
white stones,
but it's too long
to be stones!'

said Tog.

'Let's keep digging
and find out,'

said Tig and
Tog together.

After a lot of searching,
Tig and Tog found a
wheelbarrow ...

... and a BIG shovel.

With the big shovel, Tig and Tog were able to dig deeper,
and they could move more earth with the wheelbarrow.

But even the wheelbarrow and shovel weren't enough!

They STILL needed something else
to dig the thing out of the ground.

All day long Tig and Tog worked together, using all the tools they had found.

They scratched, scooped, dug, tipped and shovelled the earth around.

But even with all these
tools and all their hard
work, they still needed
something else to dig the
thing out of the ground!

Suddenly, Tog had a brilliant idea!
Leaving Tig scratching her head,
Tog soon returned with a big yellow digger!

With three mighty shovels,
the digger cleared the earth!

Tig and Tog both looked on
in amazement at what they
had found ...

It was the most ENORMOUS
dinosaur skeleton!

And the stick?

Tig decided to share the stick with Tog.
After all, she couldn't have made
the discovery without him.

And from that day on, the two friends
always shared everything.

STEGOSAURUS

FOUND BY TIG AND TOG
WITH A STICK